NICKELODEON

SpongeBob SquarePants

SpongeBob's
Special Delivery

Special Delivery! • Show Me the Bunny!
The Song That Never Ends • Camp SpongeBob
UFO! • Trouble at the Krusty Krab!

SIMON AND SCHUSTER/NICKELODEON

Based on the TV series *SpongeBob SquarePants* created by Steven Hillenburg
as seen on Nickelodeon

Stephen Hillenburg

SIMON AND SCHUSTER
First published in Great Britain in 2008 by Simon & Schuster UK Ltd
Africa House, 64-78 Kingsway, London WC2B 6AH
A CBS Company

Originally published in the USA as *SpongeBob's Ready-Read-Treasury* in 2005
by Simon Spotlight, an imprint of Simon & Schuster Children's Division, New York.

A CIP catalogue record for this book is available from the British Library

ISBN   978-1-84738-314-3

Printed in Italy

1 3 5 7 9 10 8 6 4 2

Special Delivery!

by Steven Banks
illustrated by Vince DePorter

SpongeBob was eating breakfast
at the kitchen table.
"Gary, look!" he said to his snail.
"I can get a free toy if I mail in
one hundred box tops!"
"Meow," said Gary.

So SpongeBob sat down
and ate one hundred boxes of cereal!

When he was finished eating,
SpongeBob ran to the post office
to send away for the toy.
"Now all I have to do is
go home and wait,"
said SpongeBob.

7

SpongeBob's best friend, Patrick,
came outside.

"What are you doing?" he asked.

"I am waiting!" said SpongeBob.

"Oh, boy!" cried Patrick.

"Can I wait too?"

"Sure!" replied SpongeBob.

SpongeBob and Patrick
waited by the mailbox.
"It's fun to wait!" said Patrick.
"It sure is!" agreed SpongeBob.

The next morning
Squidward saw SpongeBob and
Patrick waiting by the mailbox.
"What are you two doing out here?"
asked Squidward.
"We are waiting," replied Patrick.
"For what?" asked Squidward.
"I do not know!" said Patrick.

Squidward came outside.
"We are waiting for my free toy,"
explained SpongeBob.
"Oh, I thought we were waiting
for Santa Claus," said Patrick.

Just then the mailman walked up.
"Mr. Mailman, may I please
   have my free toy?" asked SpongeBob.
"Are you crazy?" said the mailman.
"You just mailed in for it yesterday!"

Squidward looked at the cereal box. "SpongeBob, it takes weeks for your stupid toy to arrive!" he cried.

"Haven't we been waiting
for weeks?" asked Patrick.
"You have only been out here
for one night!" said Squidward.

"I will not leave this spot until I get my toy!" said SpongeBob.

"And I will stay by your side!"
said his loyal friend Patrick.
"We have not yet begun to wait!"
cried SpongeBob.

SpongeBob and Patrick waited.

And they waited.

Then they waited some more.

And they kept on waiting!

And then one day the mailman said,
"Here's your free toy."
"At last!" cried SpongeBob.
"I knew it would come!"
"And it got here so quickly!"
Patrick added.

"Open it! Open it!" cried Patrick.
"Wait," said SpongeBob.
"Let's go tell Squidward it's here.
He will not want to miss this!"
They ran to Squidward's house.

Squidward was practicing his
clarinet in the bathtub.
"Hey, Squidward, I got my free toy!"
said SpongeBob.
"Do you want to see it?"
"No!" said Squidward.
"But I am sure you will
show it to me anyway."

SpongeBob opened the box carefully
and pulled out a piece of red string.
"Here it is!" cried SpongeBob.
"My amazing free toy!"

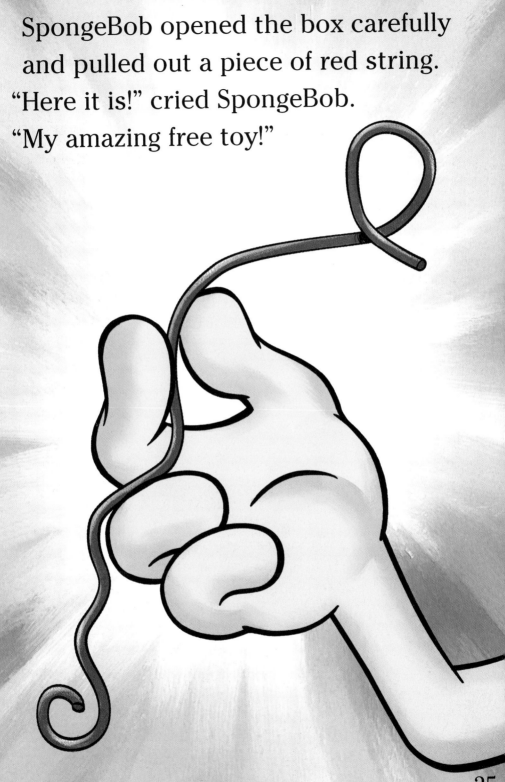

"You waited all that time
   for a stupid piece of string?"
   asked Squidward.
"Yes, but it's red! And it's free!
   And it's mine!" said SpongeBob.
Squidward just shook his head,
   while SpongeBob ran around
   and played with his piece of string.

"Can I play with it?" asked Patrick.
"Okay, but be very careful,"
  said SpongeBob.
"I waited a long time for this toy."
"You did?" asked Patrick.
  As soon as he took the string,
  it broke!

SpongeBob began to cry.
"My free toy! It's broken!"
"I am sorry, SpongeBob," said Patrick.
"It was an accident!"
"Serves you right
for wasting all that time
waiting for a cheap toy,"
said Squidward.

"He was a good little toy,"
SpongeBob said, sniffling.
"He was just too beautiful
for this cruel world.
Rest in pieces, little string."

Squidward looked out his window.
SpongeBob and Patrick were having
a service for the broken toy.
"Those losers," he said.
"Their crying is going to
keep me up all night!"

Squidward sneaked outside after dark
and dug up the little box.
"Thief!" cried SpongeBob
as Patrick shined his flashlight
on Squidward.
"Calm down, SpongeBob. It's just me,"
said Squidward.

Squidward took out the string
and tied the pieces together.
"See, it's as good as new."

"Squidward, you fixed it! You fixed
it for me!" cried SpongeBob.
"How can I ever thank you?"
"Just go home and be quiet!"
said Squidward as he
stomped back into his house.

"I know how we can thank him,"
SpongeBob told Patrick.
"We can send away for another toy!"
So they did, and they waited
right outside his window
for a long, long, long, long time!

Show Me the Bunny!

by Steven Banks
illustrated by C.H. Greenblatt and William Reiss

Knock! Knock!

"Who's there?" asked Patrick.

"It's me, SpongeBob! Guess what?
   The Easter Bunny is coming tomorrow!"

Patrick jumped up and down.
"Oh, boy, the Easter Bunny! Is he
going to come down the chimney
and bring me presents?"

PUT
GIFTS
HERE!

SpongeBob shook his head.
"No, Patrick. That's Santa Claus.
The Easter Bunny hides eggs and
we find them."

Patrick ran to his refrigerator and
grabbed a carton of eggs.
"I found the Easter eggs!" he shouted.
"Easter is tomorrow," said SpongeBob.
"Besides, Easter eggs are
painted pretty colors."

That night Patrick hung a stocking
above his fireplace and went to bed
early. SpongeBob was so excited
for Easter that he counted eggs until
he fell asleep.

Early the next morning the Easter Bunny arrived and began hiding eggs. He was about to put the first one under Patrick's rock when the noise stirred Patrick out of his deep sleep.

"Ahhhhh!" screamed Patrick. "Go away, you big, cute, fluffy monster!" The Easter Bunny was so scared that he swam away without leaving any eggs! Patrick returned to bed, proud of himself for scaring the monster away.

Whirrr! SpongeBob's alarm clock woke him up. "I have to go get Patrick! It's time for the egg hunt!"

Patrick proudly told SpongeBob how he saved Bikini Bottom from being attacked by a giant monster.

When Patrick described the "monster,"
SpongeBob said, "Oh, no, you scared
away the Easter Bunny!"
Patrick began to cry.
"I ruined Easter!"

SpongeBob asked Gary what to do.
"Meow!" replied Gary.
"You are right! I will color eggs
and hide them so Patrick's Easter
will not be ruined!" said SpongeBob.

"Patrick will never know it's me
in this Easter Bunny costume,"
SpongeBob said with a giggle.

Then he darted around, hiding
Easter eggs everywhere.
"I will put one here and here and
here and here!" cried SpongeBob.

49

When SpongeBob was done
he knocked on Patrick's rock.
Patrick looked outside and cried,
"Merry Christmas, Easter Bunny!"

"You mean 'Happy Easter,' Patrick,"
said SpongeBob, correcting him.
"Okay then, 'Happy Easter, Patrick!'"
repeated Patrick.
"Never mind," said SpongeBob. "It's
time to get your best friend and
go on an egg hunt."

SpongeBob ran home and took off his costume. Suddenly Patrick burst in. "SpongeBob, the Easter Bunny came! I am going to win the egg hunt—I can feel it!"

"It's not a contest, Patrick," said
SpongeBob. "We just find the eggs
and then eat them."
Patrick ran out the door. "I am
going to win!" he yelled.

SpongeBob and Patrick began hunting
for Easter eggs.
Soon SpongeBob's basket was full,
but Patrick could not even find
the eggs right in front of him!

SpongeBob secretly put some of his
eggs into Patrick's basket.
"Look! I found some eggs in my
basket!" cried Patrick happily.
"Now we both have eggs,"
said SpongeBob.

"Boy, all this work sure has made me hungry!" said Patrick.
He then ate all the eggs in his basket. As soon as they were gone he began to cry. "All my eggs are gone! I lost the contest! This is the worst Easter ever!"

SpongeBob felt sorry for Patrick.
"You can have some of my eggs."
Patrick smiled. "Really?"
"Sure," said SpongeBob.
Patrick took *all* of SpongeBob's eggs
and ran home shouting, "I have the
most eggs! I win!"

SpongeBob went home and cried.
"Gary, I gave all of our eggs away!
That means no egg sandwiches,
no egg pancakes, and no egg creams!"
"Meow," said Gary sadly.

Just then Patrick knocked on
the door.

"Go away!" cried SpongeBob.

"I am not in the mood for company
right now, Patrick. You took all of
my Easter eggs!"

"But I brought them back," said Patrick. "Thanks for giving them to me, but I do not need them anymore."

"Why not?" SpongeBob asked.

"Because I found the biggest Easter egg ever!" said Patrick.

SpongeBob looked up at the huge egg.
"Isn't it beautiful!" cried Patrick.
"I do not think that's an Easter
    egg," said SpongeBob.

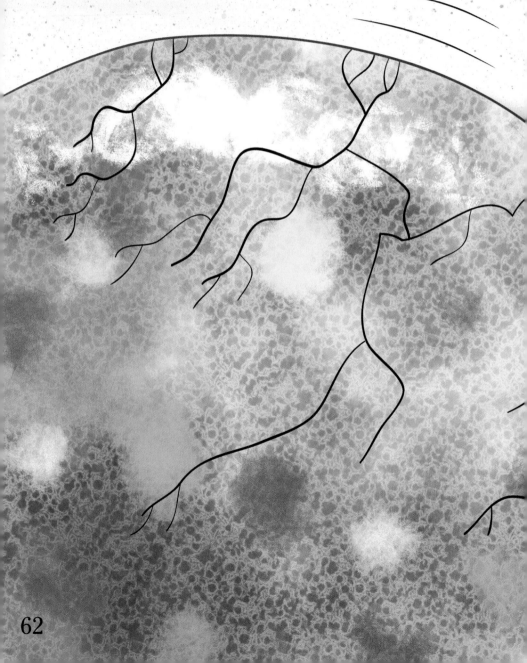

Suddenly the egg began to crack
and out came . . .

. . . a giant fish! It began
to chase them. "Run for your life!"
yelled SpongeBob.
"Merry Christmas, Easter Fishy!"
said Patrick as they ran off
into the sunset.

The Song That Never Ends

by Steven Banks
illustrated by Vince DePorter

SpongeBob SquarePants and his
friend Patrick heard strange noises
coming from their neighbor
Squidward's house.
"Out!" shouted Squidward.
"Out, I say!"

"Squidward is in trouble!"
said SpongeBob.
"Call the police!"

Patrick started running in a circle
and yelling, "Police! Police!"
SpongeBob ran to Squidward's house.

Squidward was throwing things away
in a trash can. "Out with it all!"
"I will save you!" shouted SpongeBob.
"From what?" asked Squidward.
"I am just cleaning out my closet."

"Oh, I thought you were in trouble,"
said SpongeBob.
Squidward sighed. "The only trouble
I have is you bothering me!
Now, leave me alone so I can finish!"

SpongeBob looked in Squidward's
trash can and saw a little toy guitar.
"Why are you throwing this away?"
he asked.
"It's just an old toy I played with
when I was a kid," said Squidward.

"It's broken, but it used to play
  a silly little song."
"Can I have it?" asked SpongeBob.
"Sure," said Squidward. "It's a
  worthless piece of junk!"

"Thank you, Squidward!"
said SpongeBob. "If you ever want
to visit your guitar,
just drop in anytime."
"Fine, SpongeBob," said Squidward.
"I will keep that in mind. Now go."

SpongeBob popped his head in
Squidward's window.
"If you change your mind
it will be right next door!
You know where to find us!"
"GO AWAY!" yelled Squidward.

When SpongeBob and Patrick got home,
SpongeBob fixed the toy guitar.
He turned the crank
and out came music.
"What a beautiful song,"
said SpongeBob.

"I could listen to it all day long!"
"Me too!" agreed Patrick.
   So they did.

Squidward stuck his head
out the window. "SpongeBob!
Stop playing that song!
It's driving me crazy!"

"Okay, Squidward," said SpongeBob.
"I'll stop for today."

"But I want a turn!"
complained Patrick.
SpongeBob handed him
the little guitar.

"You can play the song one
more time."
Patrick was so excited, he turned
the crank too hard and it broke off.
But the song kept playing!

Squidward banged on SpongeBob's door.
"I said, stop playing that song!"

SpongeBob tried as hard as he could,
but he could not stop the song.
"I am calling the police!"
Squidward shouted.

"What now?" asked the policeman.
"Arrest this sponge and stop
that song!" demanded Squidward.
"I like that song," said the
policeman. "My mother used to hum it
when she tucked me in at night.
SpongeBob, you can play that song
as much as you like!"

The song kept playing all night long.
Squidward put a pillow over his head,
but he could still hear it.
"I can't take it anymore!"
said Squidward. "I have got to stop
that song once and for all!"

Squidward quietly snuck into
SpongeBob's house. SpongeBob was
sound asleep, holding the guitar
in his hands.
Squidward grabbed the guitar and
SpongeBob woke up.

"Squidward, what are you doing?"
"Uh, nothing," replied Squidward.
SpongeBob smiled.

"I understand. You miss your little guitar. You were only pretending to hate the song. Here. Take it."

"I fooled SpongeBob!"
shouted Squidward as he ran outside.
Squidward raised the guitar in
the air and smashed it on a rock!
Smash! Smash! Smash!
The song finally stopped.
"I did it!" cried Squidward.

SpongeBob ran out and looked at
the busted guitar.
"Squidward, you destroyed that poor,
helpless guitar. What did it
ever do to you?"
"It kept playing that horrible song!"
said Squidward. "Now I never have
to hear it again! Ever!"

A policeman pulled up and handed
Squidward a ticket.
"It's against the law to smash a
guitar at two in the morning!
You are disturbing the peace!
That's a one-hundred-dollar fine!"

Just then a man appeared.
"My name is Fender Gibson. I collect
rare toy guitars. I thought you
might like to know that you just
smashed a one-of-a-kind
Straticastius guitar that would have
been worth a million dollars!"

93

"Look, Squidward!" said SpongeBob.
"I found the music box
   that plays the song!"
He turned the crank. "It still works!
You do not have a million dollars,
   but the song will play forever!"
"NOOOO!" screamed Squidward
   as he ran away.

CAMP SPONGEBOB

by Molly Reisner and Kim Ostrow
illustrated by Heather Martinez

It was a perfect summer day
in Bikini Bottom. Sandy spent
the morning practicing her new
karate moves.
"Hiiiyaaaa! All this sunshine
makes me more energetic
than a jackrabbit after a cup
of coffee," she said.

"Hey, Sandy, where did you first
learn karate anyway?"
SpongeBob asked.
Sandy told her friend about her days
at Master Kim's Karate Camp.

". . . and I won the championship!"
Sandy finished breathlessly.
SpongeBob leaped in the air.
"Camp sounds amazing!" he shouted.
"But I never got to go."

"When I was little, my dream
was to go to camp. But every summer
my parents sent me to Grandma's.
Sometimes I would pretend she was
my counselor, but I am not sure she
was cut out for camp life,"
SpongeBob said, sighing.

"Say no more, SpongeBob,"
    said Sandy. "Let's open Bikini
    Bottom's first summer camp.
    You can be my assistant."
"I can?" asked SpongeBob.
"Yes, and we can get started
    today," said Sandy.
"I am ready!" shouted SpongeBob.

Sandy gathered Squidward and
Patrick to tell them about the camp.
"Oh, please," Squidward said,
moaning. "Camp is for children."
"Exactly!" shouted SpongeBob.
"It would be for all the little
children of Bikini Bottom."

"Hmmm," Squidward thought out loud.
"Perhaps I could teach the
kids around here a thing or two.
Everyone would look up to me."

104

"That sounds like lots of fun,"
said Patrick. "When I was at starfish
camp, we used to lie around in the sun
and sleep a lot. I could teach
everyone how to do that!"

"I will teach karate!"
declared Sandy, kicking the air.

"Now go on home and practice
what you are going to teach.
Let's meet back here tomorrow,"
said Sandy.

The next day SpongeBob woke up
in the best mood ever.
"To be a good assistant, I need
to make sure I am prepared
with good camper activities,"
he told Gary.
SpongeBob thought of making Krabby
Patties and having bubble-blowing
contests. He imagined whole days
spent jellyfishing.

SpongeBob ran around his house
gathering all the items he needed.
"Whistle! Check. Megaphone! Check.
Visor! Check. Clipboard?"
Gary slithered over
to SpongeBob's bed and meowed.
"Good job, Gary! Check!"

SpongeBob went over to the mirror
and raised his arms. "Camping
assistants need to be strong!"
he reminded himself
as he flexed his muscles.
"Now I am ready!"

SpongeBob ran over
to the treedome.
Sandy was chopping
wood with her bare hands.
"SpongeBob SquarePants reporting
for duty!" he said, blowing his
whistle three times.

"As a good assistant, I request permission to check on everyone to make sure they are practicing their duties."

"Go for it, SpongeBob," said Sandy.

First SpongeBob went to Patrick's
rock. He watched quietly as Patrick
practiced the art of sleeping.
Then SpongeBob blew his whistle.
Patrick jumped up.
"Just making sure you are working
  hard," explained SpongeBob.
"Now go back to sleep!"

Next SpongeBob peeked
inside Squidward's house.
"I can't hear you," sang SpongeBob.
"Practice makes perfect."

SpongeBob went back to see Sandy,
who was working on her karate moves.
"All counselors are working hard,"
reported SpongeBob.
"Now what should I do?"

"Take a load off and have some
   lemonade," suggested Sandy.
"No time for lemonade,"
   said SpongeBob. "As your assistant,
   I am here to assist.
   How can I assist?"

"Listen, little buddy," said Sandy.
"You are acting nuttier than a bag
of walnuts at the county fair.
This camp is supposed to be fun."
"I will make sure it is fun!
With my assistance, this will be
the best camp ever!" SpongeBob said,
cheering.

"Attention, counselors, please
report to me right away,"
SpongeBob said. They all ran to him.
"Now go back to your posts and
PRACTICE! Camp opens tomorrow."

That night SpongeBob was so
excited, he could not sleep.
He decided to visit all
the counselors just to make sure
they were ready.

"Squidward," he whispered.
Squidward was fast asleep.
SpongeBob blew his whistle.
"Just making sure you are all
set for tomorrow."
"You are killing me, SpongeBob,"
said Squidward, and he went
back to sleep.

The next morning a very annoyed
Squidward and sleepy Patrick
headed over to Sandy's treedome.
"What are we going to do about
SpongeBob?" asked Squidward.
"I refuse to be ordered around
by him anymore."

"I have just the thing
   for the little guy," said Sandy.

"To express our gratitude
for all your hard work, we have a
small present for you," said Sandy.
"For me?" asked SpongeBob.
SpongeBob opened the box.
Inside was a camp uniform.

124

"We would like you to be the very
first camper," said Sandy.
"But don't you need me to work?"
asked SpongeBob.
"Nope. We were all so busy preparing
for camp that we never advertised
for campers! You are our first
and only camper!" exclaimed Sandy.

SpongeBob put on his uniform.
"SpongeBob SquarePants
reporting to camp!" he shouted,
running to his counselors.
"I am ready!"

by Adam Beechen   illustrated by Zina Saunders

"Grow, flower, grow!
Grow, flower, grow!"
SpongeBob and his best friend,
Patrick, sang as they marched
through SpongeBob's garden.

"What are you two
weirdos doing?"
Squidward asked.

"If you talk to plants,
   they grow fast," Patrick told him.
"And if we sing to my daffodils,
   they should grow even faster!"
SpongeBob added.

Squidward was about to tell them
to be quiet, when suddenly . . .

something very big blocked
out the light from above!

Everyone in Bikini Bottom met
to talk about what had happened.
They decided aliens must be
invading Bikini Bottom.

"We should run and hide!"
someone shouted.
"No, we should hide and then run!"
someone shouted back.

Patrick got scared and ran around
in circles.
"I do not know whether to run or
hide!" he cried.

Squidward headed to his house.
"I do not think it's the
end of the world," he grumbled.
"Everyone should go home and stop
making so much noise!"

"Maybe this is not the end
of the world," Sandy suggested.
"Maybe it's just something we do
not understand yet."

"If Sandy is not scared,
then neither am I,"
SpongeBob said.

"If you are not scared, then
I will try not to be scared either,"
Patrick told his friends.
"Well, we are scared,"
everyone else said.
"And we are going to
run and hide!"

"What are we going to do?"
SpongeBob asked.
"I think we should find out
what is making that shadow,"
Sandy told him.

THIS MIGHT
BE IT!!!

SALE!

"We can use my rocket ship
to take us to the Outer Waters
so we can get a closer look,"
Sandy said.

The friends gathered everything
they would need for their trip.
"Why do we need sandwiches?"
Sandy asked Patrick.
"Rockets make me hungry,"
Patrick explained.

They climbed into the rocket ship.
"Buckle up, fellas. It is going
to be a bumpy ride!" Sandy shouted
as they blasted off.

Patrick buckled in his sandwiches.

They saw all sorts of creatures
they had never seen before.
Patrick was a little scared,
but he tried to be brave
like SpongeBob and Sandy.

Back in his house in Bikini Bottom,
Squidward suddenly realized
how quiet it was outside.
He had not been scared of the
shadow before, but he was now.

Suddenly there was a loud knock
at his door!

"Squidward!" Mrs. Puff shouted
from the other side of the door.
"Are you sure you do not want
to come hide with us?"

"No," Squidward yelled back.
"I am not scared! I am busy playing
my clarinet!"
He tried to play his clarinet,
but he was so scared, it sounded
even worse than usual!

When Mrs. Puff and Mr. Krabs left,
Squidward quickly hid under his bed.
"I am not letting the end of the world
get me . . . or my clarinet!" he said.

Sandy's rocket soared closer
and closer to the shadow.
Patrick became more and more scared.
He could not help it.

"What if that shadow really is the end of the world?" Patrick asked. "Then at least we will have seen it up close," SpongeBob answered. "And we will have seen it together," Sandy agreed.

Finally, they were close enough
to see what was making the shadow—
and they could not believe it!

"Hey, guys," said their old friend
 Stan the manta.
"I am back from school
 to visit Bikini Bottom!"
"Wow! You got big," Sandy gasped.

"Why are you up here blocking all
the light?" Sandy asked. "You really
spooked everybody!"
"I am sorry," Stan told them.
"I could not remember
where I used to live."

"We will show you the way,"
SpongeBob said.
"Everyone will be happy to see you!"
"Especially since you are not
the end of the world," Patrick said.
No one was happier than he was!

Everyone was very happy to see Stan
again. They celebrated by playing
a new game Patrick made up called
run-and-hide-and-seek.

Squidward did not play along.
If he had played, he would have won.
He stayed in his hiding place
for two weeks!

TROUBLE AT THE KRUSTY KRAB!

adapted by Steven Banks
illustrated by Zina Saunders
based on the movie written by Derek Drymon, Tim Hill, Steve Hillenburg,
Kent Osborne, Aaron Springer, and Paul Tibbitt

There was trouble
at the Krusty Krab!
Police helicopters
circled above town.
The people of Bikini Bottom
had gathered to see
what was going on.

News reporters came up to
the owner, Mr. Krabs.
"The people want to know:
What is going on?"
asked a reporter.

"Settle down! Please!"
shouted Mr. Krabs.
"We have a problem here
    that I would rather not discuss
    until my manager gets here!"

Just then a car pulled up,
and out stepped
SpongeBob SquarePants.
The crowd cheered!

"My manager is here!"
cried Mr. Krabs with a sigh
of relief. "The day is saved!
He will know what to do!"

165

"Talk to me, Krabs,"
said SpongeBob.
"It started out as a simple order:
a Krabby Patty with cheese,"
said Mr. Krabs.

166

"So what went wrong?"
asked SpongeBob.
"The customer took a bite
and . . . and . . . and . . ."
Mr. Krabs couldn't go on.

"Spit it out, Krabs!"
   cried SpongeBob.
"THERE WAS NO CHEESE!"
   shouted Mr. Krabs
   as he started to cry.
"Get a hold of yourself, Eugene,"
   cried SpongeBob.

SpongeBob faced the crowd.
"Okay, everyone," said SpongeBob,
"I am going in."
Patrick ran up to SpongeBob
and begged, "Do not do it!
It's too dangerous!"
SpongeBob smiled. "Do not worry.
'Dangerous' is my middle name!"

As SpongeBob walked up
to the door he said,
"If I do not make it back alive,
give all my jellyfishing nets
to Squidward."
"I do not want them!"
yelled Squidward from the crowd.

The crowd watched as SpongeBob
entered the Krusty Krab.
"Will SpongeBob be able to get
some cheese on that patty,
Mr. Krabs?" asked a reporter.

"He has to! He must!" said Mr. Krabs.
"But what if he can't?"
 asked the reporter.
"THEN THE WORLD AS WE KNOW IT
 IS OVER!" cried Mr. Krabs.

The customer who had
ordered the Krabby Patty sat
in the corner of the restaurant.
He looked up at SpongeBob.
"Who are you?" he asked.
"I am the manager of this place,"
said SpongeBob.

"I am really scared, man!"
cried the customer.
SpongeBob replied, "Do not worry.
Everything is going to be fine."

Outside, the crowd waited.
A reporter spoke into a microphone
saying, "SpongeBob has been
inside for ten seconds!"
"The suspense is killing me!"
cried Mr. Krabs.
"Me too," said Patrick,
eating an ice-cream cone.

Back inside, SpongeBob sat down with
the customer. "Do you have a name?"
asked SpongeBob.
"My name is Phil," said the customer.
SpongeBob nodded and said,
"That's a good name."

"YOU DO NOT UNDERSTAND!"
screamed Phil.
"I CANNOT TAKE IT! THERE WAS
NO CHEESE!"

"Stay with me, Phil!"
  said SpongeBob.
"Do you have a family?"
"Yes," replied Phil.
"I have a lovely wife
  and two great children."
"That's what it is all about,"
  said SpongeBob.

"Okay, Phil," said SpongeBob.
"Stay calm. I am just going to
open my briefcase."
"Why?" cried Phil.
"I have only got one shot at this,
and I have to get out the
right tools for the job,"
said SpongeBob.

SpongeBob reached into the
briefcase and pulled out a pair of
solid gold tweezers.
"Solid gold tweezers!" shouted Phil.
"Yes, they are!"
said SpongeBob.

"Now I want you to do me
   a favor, Phil,"
said SpongeBob.
"What?" Phil asked.
"Say cheese!" said
   SpongeBob as he pulled
   out a slice of . . .
   CHEESE!

SpongeBob carefully put the cheese onto the Krabby Patty.

Success! The cheese was on
the Krabby Patty!
SpongeBob marched out of the
Krusty Krab with a smiling Phil
by his side.
"Order up!" cried SpongeBob.

"SpongeBob, I would like to give you the Manager of the Year Award!" said Mr. Krabs. SpongeBob just smiled back, looking pleased with himself.

Then Mr. Krabs turned to Phil
and said, "And that will be
two dollars and ninety-five cents
for the Krabby Patty, Phil."

Suddenly the crowd gathered around
SpongeBob and lifted him up
in the air.
"Three cheers for the manager!"
cried Mr. Krabs. "Hip hip!"
Honk!
"Hip, hip!" shouted Mr. Krabs.
Honk!

Honk!

Honk!

Honk!

"What's that noise?"

wondered SpongeBob.

"Sounds like an alarm clock

going off to me," said Patrick.

"It's my alarm clock!"

said SpongeBob.

"I must be dreaming!"

Honk!

SpongeBob woke up in his bed.
"Gary, I had my favorite
dream again about being the manager
of the Krusty Krab! Do you think it
will ever happen, Gary?"
"Meow," said Gary.
SpongeBob smiled.
"That is exactly how I feel!"

THE
END